bunny Overboard

Claudia Rueda

chronicle books · san francisco

Ahoy!

It's all hands on deck!
Would you like to sail
away with me?

Let's get underway!
But . . . where is the wind?

Maybe you could make some!
Would you please

blow

into the sail?

Ahh. Thank you.

Now what?
Maybe you can

rock

the book back and forth
to make waves.

Woo-hoo! Can you

rock

a bit more?

Uh-oh!

Steady as she goes.

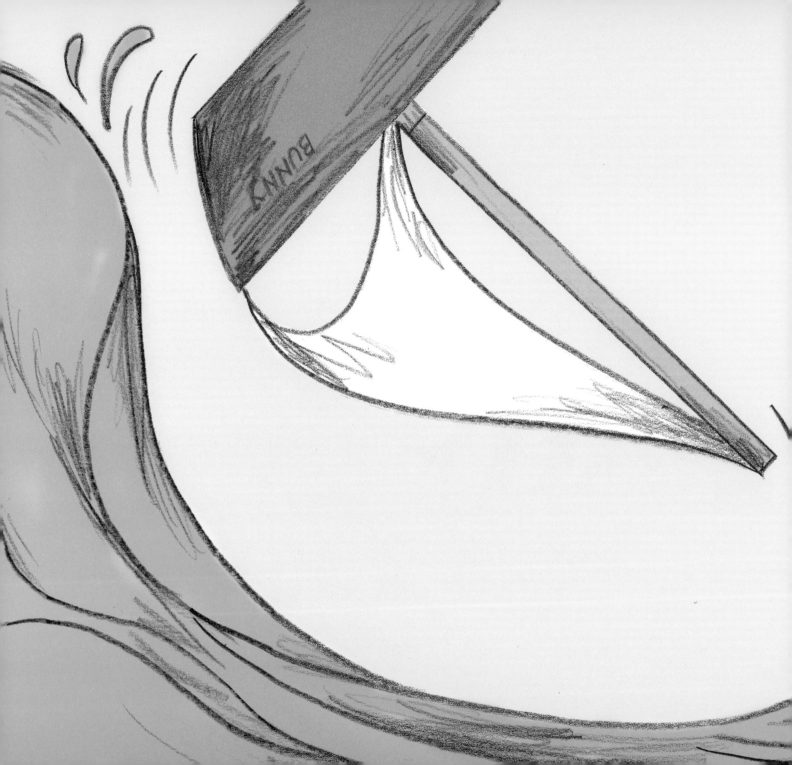

Bunny overboard!

Quick!

Stop rocking!

Kerplunk.

Phew. Maybe we'd
better stop here.

I'll just grab my gear.
We might spot something interesting!

Say it with me:

ready...set...

buns
away!

What will we see?

Ooh! What's this odd rock?
You
touch
it.

Oh! Hello, Octopus.

Would you

wipe

this ink away so we
can see again?

Look! Here's a friendly fish.
Would you give it a

pat

hello?

Oops! We didn't mean to scare you, Blowfish.

Let's float on! What do you think we'll see next?

Seven seas!
A shipwreck.

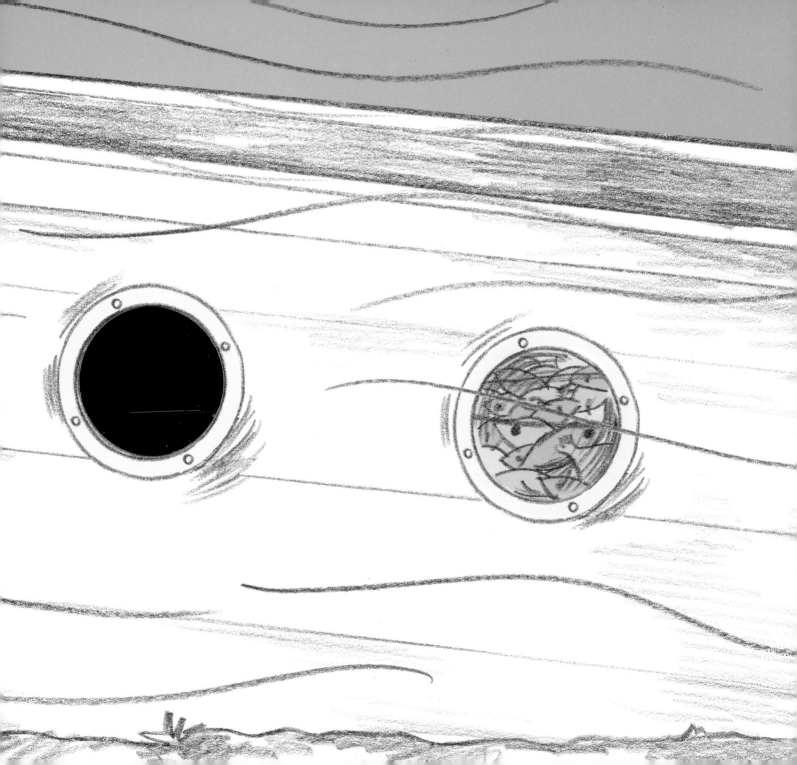

We startled
the fish!

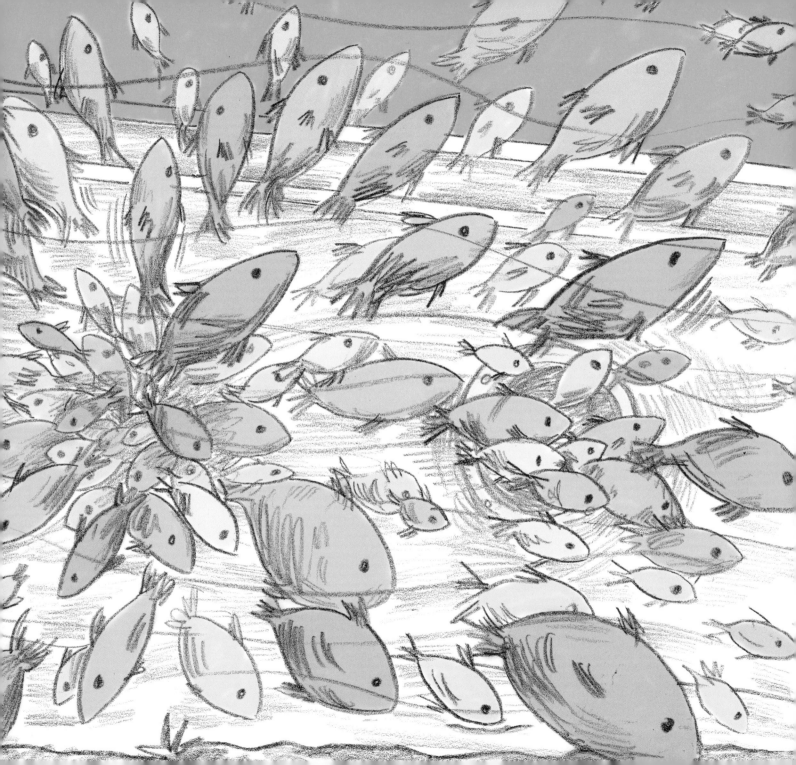

A shell! Would you **tap** to see what's inside?

It's a pearl!
What a treasure we've found.

I'm ready to be high and dry.

I see the boat! All aboard.

Anchors aweigh!

Would you help me

blow

wind in the sails
one more time?

Thank you!
And let me know if you see any
other animals on the way back.

A seal? Where is it?

There you are! I'm so glad
we found one another.

What a great day
at sea! Now it's time
to cool down with
some carrot lemonade.

And here's one for you!

Bunny would like to dedicate this book to **you**,
for all your help at sea today.

Also dedicated to Haddock, the little boat.
—Claudia

Library of Congress Cataloging-in-Publication Data available.
ISBN 978-1-4521-6256-0

Manufactured in China.

Design by Amelia Mack.
Typeset in Sprout.
The illustrations in this book were rendered in charcoal and digitally.

10 9 8 7 6 5 4 3 2

Chronicle Books LLC
680 Second Street
San Francisco, California 94107
www.chroniclekids.com